Scene

Will Smith

Dave Stern

Aladdin Paperbacks

First Aladdin Paperbacks edition
January 1999

Cover photo: ©1997
by Steve Granitz/Retna Ltd.

Text copyright ©1999
by 17th Street Productions
Threads page by Stacie Amador

Produced by 17th Street Productions,
a division of Daniel Weiss Associates, Inc.
33 West 17th Street
New York, NY 10011

Aladdin Paperbacks
An imprint of Simon & Schuster
Children's Publishing Division
1230 Avenue of the Americas
New York, NY 10020

Designed by Michael Rivilis
Printed and bound in the
United States of America
10 9 8 7 6 5 4 3 2 1

Library of Congress
Catalog Card Number 98-73799
ISBN: 0-689-82407-6

Large...

WILL SMITH HAS COME FULL CIRCLE. WITH HIS 1998 GRAMMY WIN FOR "MEN IN BLACK," HE'S RETURNED TO THE ARENA THAT FIRST MADE HIM A STAR: MUSIC.

It's hard to believe, but it was all the way back in 1988 that Will (then better known as the "Fresh Prince") and his partner Jeff Townes ("DJ Jazzy Jeff") won the very first rap Grammy award for their song "Parents Just Don't Understand."

Enough to satisfy anyone, especially eighteen-year-old Will, right?

Wrong.

Less than two years later Will left the music world for the acting world and the TV show *The Fresh Prince of Bel-Air*. But he wasn't about to stop there. While the show was becoming a smash hit, Will used his spare time to take on supporting roles in such movies as *Where the Day Takes You, Made in America,* and *Six Degrees of Separation*.

Was Will satisfied yet? Nah, far from it. He then tackled his first starring role in *Bad Boys,* an action thriller that took in over $138 million at the box office.

But he was still just getting warmed up.

Will's next movie was 1996's *Independence Day,* one of the top-grossing films of all time. A year later he followed up with another sci-fi megahit, *Men in Black*.

Charge & in

You could say that Will was on a roll. You could also say that he had become a superstar. A *major* superstar.

It was then that Will returned to music. And in typical Will Smith fashion, he didn't let his fans down. His first solo record, 1997's *Big Willie Style,* earned him yet another Grammy.

Will Smith is living life as large as it gets. Everything he touches seems to turn to gold. How do people explain his phenomenal popularity?

"Will's funny, self-confident . . . good-looking. . . . [He's got] that movie star thing going," says Barry Sonnenfeld, the director of *Men in Black.*

Will has a different answer.

"It's the ears," he says, smiling.

HOW BIG ARE WILL'S EARS? A FRIEND ONCE DESCRIBED WILL AS LOOKING LIKE "A '68 BUICK WITH THE DOORS OPEN."

"Americans have an ear fetish. Mickey Mouse, Goofy, Ross Perot—they love people with big ears."

Well . . . maybe. But Will has some other qualities that might better explain his success. For one, he's a pleasure to work with.

"I never want to do a movie without Will Smith again," says Sonnenfeld.

For another, he works harder than anyone else.

"No one else is going to put in the hours I put in," Will says. "I have this really psychotic drive. I can't sleep, I can't eat until what I start is finished to the best of my ability."

Where did such a hardworking, good-natured, old-fashioned kind of nice guy come from?

The short answer is Philadelphia.

But if you really want to find Will Smith's roots, you have to look at his role models. His heroes.

His mom and dad.

"The only people I ever idolized."

Will and Jada at the 1997 *Soul Train* Awards.

"I GREW UP IN A **BAPTIST** HOUSEHOLD, WENT TO A **CATHOLIC** SCHOOL, LIVED IN A PREDOMINATELY **JEWISH** NEIGHBORHOOD, AND HUNG WITH THE **MUSLIM** KIDS."
—Will on his diverse childhood

Big Willie's Crib

CAROLINE AND WILLARD SMITH SR. ALREADY HAD ONE CHILD—THEIR DAUGHTER PAMELA—WHEN THEY WELCOMED YOUNG WILL INTO THE WORLD ON SEPTEMBER 25, 1968.

They claim that before he could walk, Will was already mugging for the camera. A born entertainer? Will admits to it. "There I am in my parents' videotapes, days old, right in front . . . smiling away with no teeth."

A few years later, when Will Sr. and Caroline had twins (another girl, Ellen; and a brother, Harry), Will's first audience was complete. Not that he was the only one in the family who was funny—"dinnertime was a nightly laugh riot," he recalls—but Will was always the one to put things over the top.

And how, you might ask, did he do that? Well, sometimes he'd place things in his nose (his sister Ellen remembers one particular incident with a straw), and he generally just pushed the edge of acceptable behavior.

But Will quickly learned his limits because his parents were always there to set them. His mom, a school administrator, and his dad, an ex–military man turned small-business owner, knew when to draw the line.

And draw it firmly they did. They insisted on hospital corners on the bedsheets at home and good grades at school. They sent Will to Our Lady of Lourdes, a Catholic school that was a forty-minute bus ride away. At Lourdes, Will excelled in creative writing and showed genuine aptitude for math and science.

And quickly became known as the class clown.

In part, it was just his natural showmanship coming to the fore.

In part, it must have been the ears. "Everyone always told me I looked like Alfred E. Neuman, the weird guy on the cover of *Mad* magazine," Will recalls.

In ninth grade Will left Lourdes and enrolled in Overbrook, the local public high school. It was there that teachers started calling him "Prince" (short for "Prince Charming") because the excuses he made up for cutting class were so imaginative and entertaining.

It wasn't that Will got bad grades or anything, but by high school he had found something a lot closer to his heart than academics—music.

Music had always played a big part in the Smith household. Family jam sessions were a common occurrence. Will had taken piano lessons and even played in the school band for a while.

Plus the radio was always on in Will's house. Will got his first stereo when he was ten and was practically raised on '70s funk bands like Parliament and the Bar-Kays.

And then, when he was eleven years old, Will heard the Sugar Hill Gang for the first time.

That would change everything.

Threads

Want to get this look?

Jada gives gray a whole new attitude, thanks to her . . .

PRETTY EYE SHADOW IN THE SAME SLATE TONES AS HER DRESS ●

SHIMMERY LIP GLOSS ●

SOPHISTICATED GRAY BEADED DRESS ●

elegant&

Want to get Jada's look? Look for a beautiful slip dress and add a rhinestone choker, bracelet, and small earrings. Note that Jada has only one ring and one bracelet on so as not to take away from her beautiful beaded dress. So choose one or two special pieces, and you, too, will look just like a glamour girl.

Will has got it goin' on. Although he normally prefers T-shirts and shorts, he looks picture-perfect here with his . . .

● <u>SHIMMERY GRAY ASCOT</u>

● <u>MATCHING GRAY POCKET SQUARE</u>

● <u>VERY HIP SUIT</u>

The look is glamourous

Want your boyfriend to match your sophisticated look for a night on the town? Take him to any major department store, scope out the suit section for a suit that complements your dress, find a matching shirt and tie, and you're all set!

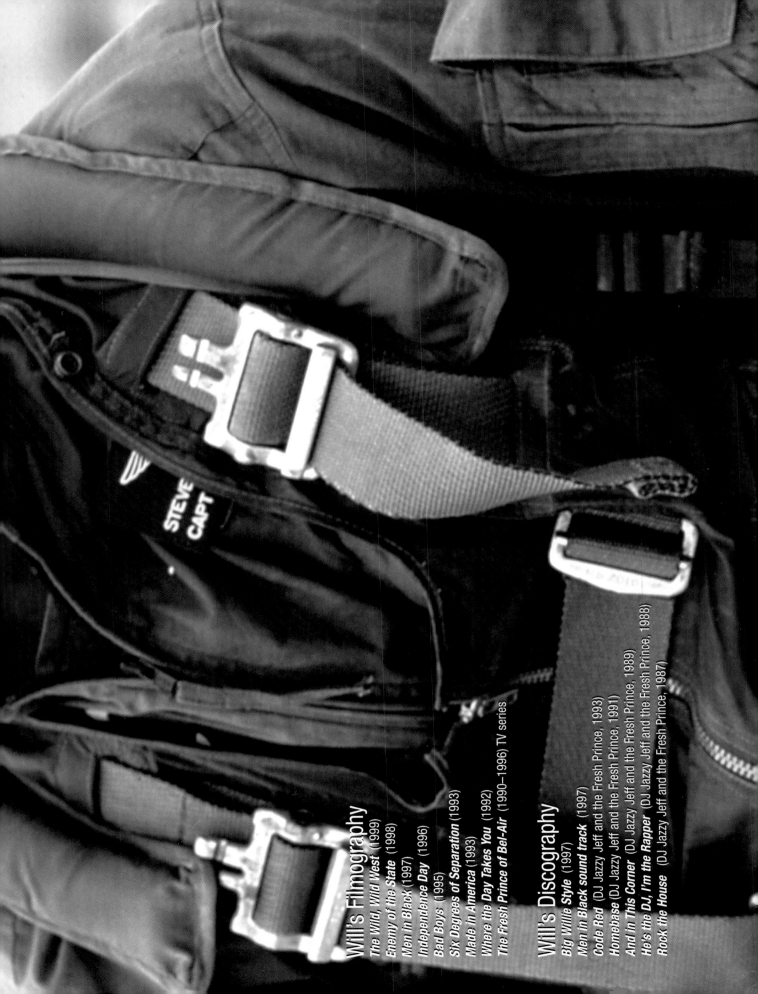

Will's Filmography

The Wild, Wild West (1999)
Enemy of the State (1998)
Men in Black (1997)
Independence Day (1996)
Bad Boys (1995)
Six Degrees of Separation (1993)
Made in America (1993)
Where the Day Takes You (1992)
The Fresh Prince of Bel-Air (1990–1996) TV series

Will's Discography

Big Willie Style (1997)
Men in Black sound track (1997)
Code Red (DJ Jazzy Jeff and the Fresh Prince, 1993)
Homebase (DJ Jazzy Jeff and the Fresh Prince, 1991)
And in This Corner (DJ Jazzy Jeff and the Fresh Prince, 1989)
He's the DJ, I'm the Rapper (DJ Jazzy Jeff and the Fresh Prince, 1988)
Rock the House (DJ Jazzy Jeff and the Fresh Prince, 1987)

A Pri

Will posing with
DJ Jazzy Jeff.

nce Is Born

IN THE EARLY 1980s RAP WASN'T THE MUSIC OF THE MAINSTREAM AS IT IS TODAY. RAP WAS SOMETHING DIFFERENT. SOMETHING NEW.

It all started in New York—in the Bronx and in Brooklyn—with two rappers busting rhymes at each other over DJ beats and quickly became the music of the urban teen. The song that let the rest of the country know about this new sound was "Rapper's Delight," by New Jersey's Sugar Hill Gang.

The groove hit eleven-year-old Will hard. But what hit him just as strongly was the realization that this new art form melded two of his passions—music and storytelling. This was something he could do.

And he did. By the time he was thirteen, Will was rapping his own songs at neighborhood parties. Showing his business savvy at a young age, Will then decided to turn his talent into some money.

"Everybody else was going to parties and having fun, and I said, 'Okay, if I'm going to a party, I might as well get paid for it.' So I became a DJ."

But before too long, Will—too much the natural performer to accept a background role—stepped out from behind the turntable and grabbed the mike once again.

Meanwhile another Philly boy by the name of Jeff Townes had also been blown away by the sounds of the Sugar Hill Gang and other early rappers. He was fascinated by technology and by the whole art of cutting up something old into pieces and making something new out of it. A big jazz fan, he longed to blend the sophistication of that music with the new hip-hop sound.

Jeff got an early start on his music career, too. Legend has it that he was working as a DJ when he was just ten. A few short years later he set up a studio in his basement to get his music down on tape. Then in 1983 local airplay of his tunes cemented Jeff's reputation as one of the emerging stars of the new hip-hop nation. He started to call himself DJ Jazzy Jeff.

But it wasn't until three years later that he and Will hooked up at a party in Will's neighborhood. Will started rapping to Jeff's beats, and before you knew it, they were a team.

DJ Jazzy Jeff and the Fresh Prince (Will took the Prince nickname his teachers had given him and made p-hop by adding the word [fres]h to it) spent every spare [mi]nute in Jeff's basement studio, writing, rehearsing, and recording.

But Will had other responsibilities in his life, too. And if he let those slide . . . well, his mom and dad were always there to remind him of them.

One of those responsibilities was school. Will buckled down; he stopped cutting class. He took the SATs and aced them.

Then he and Jeff got a record deal.

It was just for a twelve-inch single. It was only on a local label. But the song they cut,

Will with Kool Moe Dee.

"Girls Ain't Nothin' but Trouble," had the combination of elements that would later make them wildly successful: Will's humor and

storytelling sensibility mixed with Jeff's innovative and eclectic use of technology.

The song took off on local radio and became a hit in England. Will and Jeff traveled as part of the Def Jam tour with LL Cool J, Eric B. & Rakim, and Public Enemy. When they arrived in London, they were greeted like visiting royalty.

Will's first taste of success made him eager for more.

A major label picked them up and set the two of them to work on their first full-length album, *Rock the House*. When the record was released, it was an instant smash, selling over half a million copies and going gold.

But before Will could wholeheartedly throw himself into his music, he had a decision to make.

College.

It was his last year of high school, and even though his career was taking off, Will's parents had a hard time giving up their own dreams for him. He'd been accepted into several schools; interviewers from the prestigious Massachusetts Institute of Technology had even come to him, suggesting that he apply to a special scholarship program.

But Will knew what he wanted, and college didn't fit into the equation.

His mother in particular was upset by his decision. "She told all the schools I got into to hold the dorm room, just hoping I'd change my mind," Will says. But once she and his dad got a look at Will's plans for his recording group, they relented. A little.

"You can do this for a year," his dad basically told him. "If it doesn't work, then you'll go to college."

His course set, Will went back into the studio with Jeff to start work on their second full-length album. What they emerged with was the groundbreaking, two-record set (rap's first double album) *He's the DJ, I'm the Rapper*.

The first single from that was "Parents Just Don't Understand." The song was a perfect marriage of music and lyrics, message and entertainment. It wasn't hardcore. It wasn't street. But then, Will and Jeff weren't trying to be NWA or Ice-T. They were just being themselves—two kids having fun making music.

Which a lot of people had fun listening to. The single went triple platinum (that's three million discs) and won the recording industry's very first rap Grammy.

Jeff had always been recognized as one of rap's leading DJs, but now Will was getting some respect, too. Harry Allen of *Essence* magazine called Will "an incredibly imaginative lyricist and vocalist . . . true to the meaning of hip-hop music—which is vocal excellence, imagination, liveliness."

Success bred success, and Will and Jeff's next big hit, "Summertime," from the *And in This Corner* album, won them yet another Grammy in 1990.

© Nick Charles/Star File

DJ Jazzy Jeff and The Fresh Prince performing in the early days.

THE DAY THAT WILL AND JEFF GOT BACK TO PHILADELPHIA AFTER WINNING THEIR FIRST GRAMMY, JEFF'S MOTHER HUMBLED THEM BY SENDING THEM TO THE STORE TO BUY A CAN OF YAMS, A LOAF OF BREAD, AND A GALLON OF MILK.

Success also bred money. And with money life became, as Will put it, a little unreal.

He bought a big house in Philadelphia, fancy clothes, luxury cars (six of them, in fact). He and Jeff traveled around the world with the biggest posse you could imagine. He wore a gold necklace that spelled out The Fresh Prince with the T, F, and P in diamonds.

At twenty years old Will was a millionaire.

One day he called his father up to brag. He talked about the clothes, the mansion, the traveling. The six cars.

His dad stopped him right there.

"What do you need six cars for," Will Sr. asked, "when you only have one butt?"

His dad was right, of course. And a little prophetic. Instead of being so immersed in his toys Will should have been watching that one butt of his.

It was about to land hard—on the ground.

Will sitting on his throne as The Fresh Prince of Bel-Air.

Bel-

Air Bound

IT TOOK WILL EIGHTEEN YEARS TO EARN HIS FIRST MILLION DOLLARS. IT TOOK HIM LESS THAN TEN MONTHS TO LOSE IT.

You see, while Will was taking in all that money, he forgot to do one thing: set some aside to pay taxes. Put another way, the Fresh Prince was in serious debt to the government.

Will ended up having to sell most of the toys he'd bought and even moved back home for a while. He crashed back down to reality—fast.

"There's nothing more sobering than having six cars and a mansion one day and [not enough money] to buy gas the next," Will says.

But as depressing as it was, the situation gave Will a chance to examine who he was. And he decided it was time for a change. A new direction.

"I knew I wanted to entertain, so Los Angeles was the place to go," he says. He moved to a rented apartment in Burbank, trying, and failing, to convince Jeff to move out there with him. The two of them kept working on music together, but Will's new focus was on breaking into acting. Then came the meeting that would change his life.

Will was backstage at *The Arsenio Hall Show*, the hottest thing on late night TV at the time, when he bumped into a Warner Brothers exec named Benny Medina. Will and Benny got to talking, and as soon as Will mentioned that he was looking to do some acting, a little lightbulb went off above Medina's head.

For some time Medina had been wrestling with developing a sitcom. The premise was basically his life story: As a youngster, Medina had been taken in off the streets by a wealthy Bel-Air family. A classic fish-out-of-water tale.

The moment he met Will, Medina knew he'd found his on-screen alter ego. He brought entertainment biz legend Quincy Jones on board as executive producer and soon had a team working on the concept. Six months later they had a pitch meeting with NBC's Warren Littlefield.

Will's potential as a star was immediately apparent to all involved.

Medina remembers that Will "picked up this lousy script and read life into lines he had never seen before, in front of the network brass. . . . Once he was in front of the camera, he had the ability to completely capture your attention."

Will with the cast of *The Fresh Prince of Bel-Air.*

friends—and eventually much more.

But that comes later. It was another woman, Sheree Zampino, who first won Will's heart. Will met Sheree at a taping of the TV show *A Different World,* and the two married in 1992.

"She's wonderful," Smith said at the time. "She allowed me to finally put down the baggage of emotional stress I'd been lugging around like a fool."

Now it was time for Will's show to go into production. The Hollywood hype machine went into overdrive. Pollsters crowed about how the show had tested through the roof—higher even than the phenomenally successful *Cosby Show.*

There was just one problem: Will couldn't really act yet.

"The only thing that saved me on the show that first year was that everybody else was

Littlefield agrees. "Will read from the script and just nailed it. I sat there thinking, 'Just bottle this guy!'"

The show, needless to say, was picked up.

As auditions for Will's supporting cast began, one of the actresses who tried out for the part of Will's girlfriend was another relative newcomer to the Hollywood scene: Jada Pinkett.

She didn't get the part, but she still remembers their first meeting, back in 1990. It took place while she was leaving the set.

"He was like, 'What's up?' and I was like, 'Yeah, how you doing?' I was ticked off that I didn't get the job." The two of them, however, ended up becoming good

funny," he's since admitted.

The following year Will relaxed a little more. He brought Jeff on the show as a semiregular. And he became a better actor himself. In the process *The Fresh Prince of Bel-Air* became more real, funnier, and better television.

"Will's creative instincts," Medina said at the time, ". . . have turned the Will character into his own man. Now Will really is Will, reflecting all his personal charm and spontaneity. . . . *The Fresh*

"WILL SMITH IS A ROCKET SHIP. HE JUST TOOK OFF AND KEPT GOING."
—Warren Littlefield, NBC Entertainment president

Prince has emerged as a genuine comic hero, a warm and funny guy who speaks the language of young urban America."

Will not only realized he could carry the show but felt that it was his responsibility to do so.

"The truth is that I know there are millions and millions of black youths like me—kids who have never touched a drug or a drink, kids who are filled with self-esteem, kids who want to have fun, want to laugh, want to rap, want to party but aren't afraid of responsibility. Those same kids—and include me among them—are tired of the white media, especially the white news media, portraying black youths as criminals to be feared as opposed to progressive young people to be respected."

Will with Issac Hayes in *The Fresh Prince of Bel-Air.*

So, Will had grown into his role as a TV star. Now he wanted to push himself as an actor—something that came as no surprise to Benny Medina, who had since become one of Will's managers.

"Movies," Medina recalls, "were something Will said he wanted to do the first time we talked."

Keepin' It Reel

Will with Tommy Lee Jones in *Men in Black.*

EVEN BEFORE STARRING IN THE *FRESH PRINCE OF BEL-AIR*, WILL AND DJ JAZZY JEFF HAD BEEN APPROACHED FOR THE ROLES EVENTUALLY ASSIGNED TO KID N' PLAY IN THE FILM *HOUSE PARTY*.

And then he got the opportunity he'd been waiting for. He was offered a small role completely outside his Fresh Prince character. He knew he had to take it.

The film was *Where the Day Takes You*, and in it Will plays a wheelchair-bound homeless person named Manny. Though not a commercial smash, the film put the powers that be on notice: Will Smith was now an actor to be taken seriously.

Will's next movie role was in *Made in America*, a comedy that starred Whoopi Goldberg and Ted Danson. Although this movie wasn't a box office hit, either, it gave Will the confidence to go out for a meatier part.

And he knew just what that part was. The film Will wanted to star in was *Six Degrees of Separation*, the story of a well-heeled young black man who cons a wealthy, white New York City family into letting him stay with them.

He wasn't the producer's first choice for the role. He knew that going in. But that's where Will's work ethic took over.

"My drive was the fact that they didn't want me. They didn't think I could do it. They thought I was the worst choice you could have for the role. But that gave me the strength and energy to do this."

But while that drive ended up winning him the part and critical acclaim after the movie was released, it didn't come without a price.

The cost was Will's marriage—barely a year old at the time.

"I didn't know that when you work on a role that hard it gets inside of you, that it makes you crazy, puts you in a different place," Will explains. "When I was doing the character, I became him for a little while. I would block out seventy-two hours and try and shop like he would shop—just be him. Sheree and I were newlyweds, and I was crazy."

The couple had a son—Will the Third, nicknamed Trey—in 1992—but in 1995 they divorced.

Emotionally broken up, Will turned to the young woman who'd remained his friend for so many years. "Jada was there to talk to me. She took care of me."

Jada never thought that she and Will would end up in a romantic relationship. "I perceived Will as the goofy Fresh Prince on the show. . . . Every time I'd see him, that's the way he was acting."

But the more time they spent together, the more they realized they were made for each other. It's not just that they had the exact same sense of humor but that they both lived, and wanted to live, the same lifestyle.

"Actors hook up out of necessity," Will explains. "Jada being an actress . . . she understands fame, she understands fans, having money, not having money, a

Will with Donald Sutherland and Stockard Channing in *Six Degrees of Separation*.

successful creative endeavor versus an unsuccessful creative endeavor and how that affects you psychologically and emotionally."

Will's breakup with Sheree aside, most of his endeavors were proving wildly successful. *Fresh Prince* continued to climb in the ratings—in no small part due to Will's increased input on the show. And while his rap career was temporarily on hold, Will's next film let Hollywood know that a new star had arrived.

Bad Boys, which costarred comedian Martin Lawrence, was a first-class production all the way. Aside from being a huge hit,

A very bankable hunk. Scripts began to come Will's way in droves.

Still, there was a downside to Will's burgeoning film career. The Fresh Prince character now started to seem confining to him.

In 1995 Will decided that the show's sixth season would be its last. It was a bittersweet ending for Will—the sitcom's ratings were still high, he was more involved in the creative process than he'd ever been, and he'd made a lot of good friends during Fresh Prince's six years. But he wanted to end on a high note.

"I talked to Sherman Hemsley [George Jefferson on *The Jeffersons*], and he said the way that they found out that *The Jeffersons* was over is they came to the set one Monday, and their parking spaces were gone. You know, I didn't want to go out that way."

But even as he finished

Will and Martin Lawrence in *Bad Boys.*

"I TRY **NOT TO PAY** ATTENTION TO THE **BOX OFFICE.** JUST DO THE WORK. ENJOY IF IT'S A GOOD MOVIE . . . LET THAT BE ENOUGH. NOT TO HAVE TO EARN **$100 MILLION IN SEVENTEEN MINUTES.** IT'S TOO MUCH PRESSURE, AND IT REALLY IS OUT OF YOUR CONTROL."
—Will Smith

the movie also showed off a whole new Will Smith. In preparation for his role as Miami cop Mike Lowery, Will hit the gym big time. The skinny Fresh Prince, the former Alfred E. Neuman look-alike, was suddenly a hunk.

CAPT. STEVEN HILLER "EAGLE"

Will in *Independence Day.*

Will in *Independence Day.*

Will with Tommy Lee Jones and Rip Torn in *Men In Black*.

off one phase of his career Will was firmly focused on the next. He wanted to make the leap from film actor to film star.

"I looked at the top ten movies of all time," he recalls, "and seven of the ten had creatures in them. *E.T., Jurassic Park, Close Encounters, Jaws* . . . so it was like, I want to make movies that have creatures."

Cut to Dean Devlin and Roland Emmerich, cocreators of the highly successful sci-fi film

Stargate. 20th Century Fox had just given them the go-ahead to produce another sci-fi film—with creatures. Mean creatures from outer space.

In casting *Independence Day*, Devlin and Emmerich felt it was crucial that they found actors who were humorous. Both fans of Will's music videos, they were overjoyed when he signed on as a member of the cast.

Will was determined to make the most of his shot at super-

Will in *Men In Black*.

stardom. *Independence Day* was a disaster movie, so he studied the genre intensely. One performance in particular stuck in his mind: Ernest Borgnine's role as a cynical

Will as Agent J in *Men In Black*.

"HERE'S HOW I BECOME FUNNY. I STAND AS CLOSE TO WILL SMITH AS I CAN GET."

—Tommy Lee Jones

cop in one of the most classic disaster movies of all time, *The Poseidon Adventure*.

"I watched Borgnine's performance about twenty times because he was funny in a life-and-death situation. But he wasn't funny ha-ha—he was deadly serious. What I learned from Borgnine is you can stand there straight and just say a line, and let the moment make it funny."

All Will's preparation paid off.

Smith's role as Captain Steven Hiller was intended to be a minor character. But when the film literally exploded across the country, it was Will who grabbed the spotlight.

Will was now a member of Hollywood's A-list. He could pick and choose his roles. Saving the world from an alien invasion two summers in a row was not what he had in mind.

But when Stephen Spielberg calls you up and demands that you take a role in the next film he's producing, then flies you out to his Long Island estate to sell you on the idea, what actor could say no?

Certainly not Will. His next film was Spielberg's *Men in Black*. In the movie Will plays a streetwise New York City cop who discovers that aliens have existed on Earth in secret for the last fifty years. The movie was a comedy-thriller, and director Barry Sonnenfeld used Will's razor-sharp comedic timing every chance he got. Audiences loved it. The movie was an enormous success.

But even more important to his fans, *MIB* provided Will with the opportunity to get back into the arena that had first made him a star. An arena that Will often felt had completely passed him by.

"WHAT I LOVE ABOUT WILL MORE THAN ANYTHING IS THAT HE'S A ONE-WOMAN MAN. HE LOVES BEING IN LOVE AND IN A RELATIONSHIP."
—Will's *Independence Day* costar Vivica A. Fox

© Vincent Zuffante/Star File

Will and Jada with Will's son, Trey, and Will's nephew at the premiere for *Men in Black.*

Will holding up his award at the
1998 Blockbuster Awards.

ull Circle

RAP MUSIC HAD CHANGED A LOT IN THE YEARS SINCE SMITH HAD MADE HIS DEBUT. AND NOT, IN HIS OPINION, FOR THE BETTER.

"Now it seems to be completely ignorant and socially degenerate," he said in 1996. "There's nothing more unappealing than somebody with a mike standing up, abusing their right to free speech."

Will wanted to get back into music—and not just for his own sake. He had someone else's best interests in mind, too.

"My son," he told *Essence* magazine, "doesn't have any [rap] alternatives."

Will wanted to be a positive role model for Trey (who he shares custody of with ex-wife Sheree) the way his dad had been for him.

Still, it had been years since DJ Jazzy Jeff and the Fresh Prince topped the charts. People loved Will Smith, movie star, but would they respond to Will Smith, rapper?

The success of *Independence Day* and *MIB* gave Will the clout to find out. For the first time he was able to make a record without worrying about money.

"Whatever video I saw in my head; whatever producers I wanted to work with . . . this was my opportunity, with no excuses."

He brought in a number of superstar collaborators— Larry Blackmon from Cameo, Lisa "Left Eye" Lopes from TLC, Trackmasters, and, as he was quick to point out in every interview he did, DJ Jazzy Jeff, who acted as co-producer on two tracks.

On November 25, 1997, Will released his first solo record, *Big Willie Style.* No longer billing himself as the Fresh Prince, he'd clearly matured as an artist. But he didn't know if the public was going to accept him.

Will needn't have been worried. *Big Willie Style* was a hit from the word go. Successfully bridging the rap, R&B, and pop market, the record proved that in a world dominated by gangsta rap, there was always room for Will Smith's positive, feel-good energy.

The video for the album's first single, "Gettin' Jiggy wit It," was soon the most requested on MTV. And when it was released as a single, it topped the Billboard charts.

But as successful as *Big Willie Style* was, Will's high point in 1997 had to be his New Year's Eve wedding to longtime steady Jada Pinkett.

The year 1998 has been even busier for Will. He picked up his third Grammy and an MTV video award for the theme from *MIB* in the beginning of the year. Then he went to shoot *Enemy of the State,* a political thriller costarring Gene Hackman and scheduled to hit theaters in late 1998. When that

project completed filming, he went back to work with director Barry Sonnenfeld on the movie remake of an old TV show, *The Wild, Wild West,* slated to be released in summer of 1999.

And there's still more Will to come. *MIB 2* is reportedly in development, as is *The Mark,* a comedic thriller from *Independence Day* producers Devlin and Emmerich, starring Will and set against the final hours of the coming millennium. There are also rumors floating around about Will and Whitney Houston costarring in a romantic comedy titled *Anything for Love.* And if that's not enough, Will and Jada recently wrote a screenplay together called *Love for Hire.*

But for Will, all the Hollywood glamour and all the hype must pale in comparison to the July birth of his and Jada's son, Jaden Christopher Syre Smith.

How does Will keep a level head?

"I've always found that money and success don't change people; they merely amplify what is already there. I always believed in treating people well. And I still do."

Will's never been the type to stay in one place for too long. But it's hard to imagine what worlds in the entertainment industry remain for Will Smith to conquer. Perhaps he needs to look elsewhere for his dreams, to find new challenges. . . .

"I want to do everything. I want to be the first black president. Give me about ten years, I'm going to run for president. If I can squeeze in an NBA championship before that, I'll do it."

Will was smiling when he said it. Still . . .

Never bet against the Fresh Prince.

(Above) Will and Jada at the 1997 MTV Music Video Awards. (Left) Will and Gene Hackman in a scene from *Enemy of the State*.

THE LOWDOWN ON WILL

Full name: Willard Smith Jr. **Birthplace:** Philadelphia, Pennsylvania **Birth date:** September 25, 1968 **Sign:** Libra **Hair:** Brown **Eyes:** Brown **Height:** 6'3" **Weight:** 200 pounds **Heroes:** Mom and Dad **Pets:** Four Dobermans—Tyson, Gracie, Zachy, and Indo **Favorite sport:** "Golf . . . it's the perfect blend of physical ability and mental prowess." **If he hadn't been a rapper:** "I love to invent things. . . . I might have been the guy who invented the TV remote control!" **Favorite comedian:** Eddie Murphy **Dream role:** Muhammed Ali **Favorite basketball player:** Charles Barkley **Favorite food(s):** Burger and fries; fried chicken **If a restaurant had a Will Smith special, it would be:** "A big, thick, double-fudge brownie with vanilla ice cream, whipped cream, nuts, and a cherry!" **Haircut:** "A fade. I've had a fade my whole life. It's a military thing, but people in Philly started doing it for fashion." **Favorite style of music:** Dance **Singers:** Mariah Carey, Bobby Brown **Rappers:** Ice Cube, Eazy-E, The Fugees, Nas **Early inspiration:** The Sugar Hill Gang, Dr. Seuss **Grammy awards:** Three, for "Parents Just Don't Understand," "Summertime" (both with DJ Jazzy Jeff), and "Men in Black" **If he hadn't been a rapper, part two:** Will might have been a paleontologist—he loves dinosaurs! **Best learning experience:** Acting in special effects films: "It's difficult to get a performance because it's so technical. You have to get your head a certain way, then your arm has to be up a certain way when you're talking. . . . It's like, aargh!" **Best un-learning experience:** Acting in *Fresh Prince*: "I had to learn not to look at the camera. In [music] videos, that's what you do."